ANIMALS IN DANGER

RHINOS

By Emily Kington

Words that appear in **BOLD** are explained in the glossary.

First published by Hungry Tomato Ltd in 2022
F1, Old Bakery Studios, Blewetts wharf, Malpas Road, Truro, Cornwall, TR1 1QH, UK.

www.hungrytomato.com

ISBN 978-1-914087-61-5

A CIP catalog record for this book is available from the British Library.

Manufactured in the USA.

Picture credits (t=top, b=bottom, m=middle, l-left, r=right, bg=background)

Corbis:18bl, 25ml, 25mr, 25bl. **Superstock**: 10bl, 17br, 26ml. **Shutterstock**: 10-11bg, 16bg, 24br, 24mr, 4-5bg, 4bl, 8bl, Brester Irina 22bl; 29tr; Christian Edelmann 20-21bg; Emma geary 6-7bg, 32br; Erika J Mitchell 30br; Katie Sh 29m; Kirill Dorofeev 2-3bg, 31bg; Kurit Afshen 8tr, 26mr; Louise Rigolet 1bg, 27br; Maggy Meyer 28b; Maksim Safaniuk 27bl; Marcel brekelmans 18-19bg, 26bl; Michael Rads 27m; Raiyani Muharramah 8-9bg; Rewat thamlena 12-13bg; Rudi Hulshof 21tr; Sandeep-Bisht 22-23bg; Stu Porter 29bl; Sue Berry 30ml; Udo Kieslich 14-15bg; Udo Kieslich 28tr; Volodymyr Burdiak 7br.

Every effort has been made to trace the copyright holders, and we apologize in advance for any unintentional omissions. We would be pleased to insert the appropriate acknowledgements in any subsequent edition of this publication.

CONTENTS

Rhino is short for rhinoceros, which means 'nose horn'. There are five different types of rhino.

African rhinos live on the grassy plains of southern Africa. Asian rhinos live in forests and on grasslands in India and other countries in South East Asia.

All types of rhino are **endangered**. Some are already **extinct**.

An Asian female rhinoceros and her calf.

ENDANGERED & EXTINCT

An African bull (male) rhinoceros.

AFRICAN RHINOS

An African black rhino

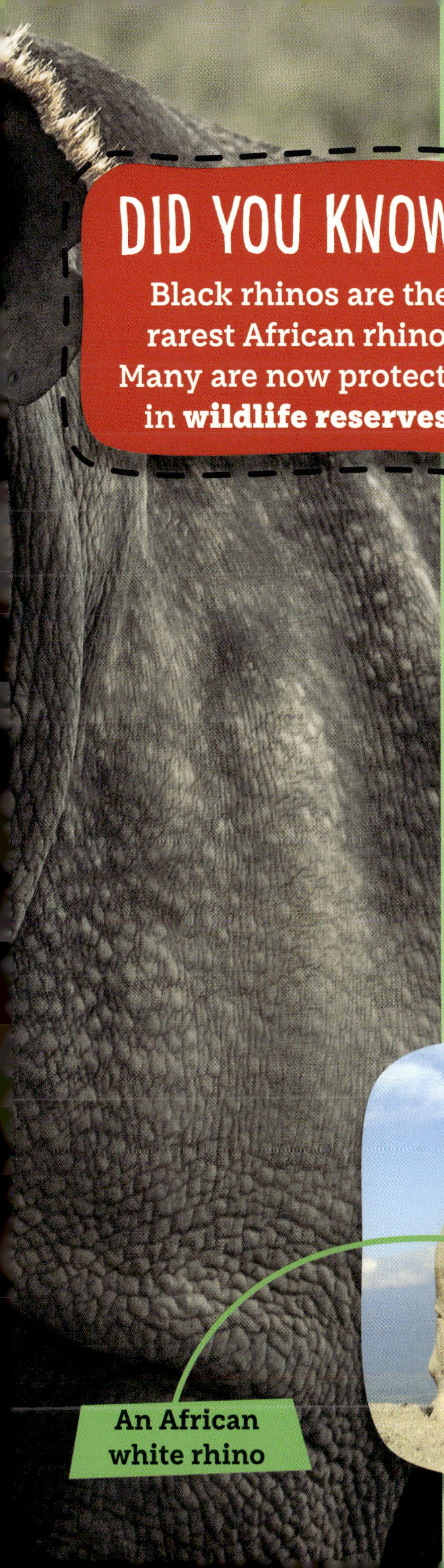

DID YOU KNOW?

Black rhinos are the rarest African rhino. Many are now protected in **wildlife reserves.**

Two sorts of rhino live in Africa, the black rhino and the white rhino. Both types are actually the same color - grey!

African rhinos live on open plains, called the **savannah**. They are plant eaters. They eat grass and leaves from low-growing bushes.

The African name for white rhinos was 'wide mouthed rhino', because they have wider mouths than the black rhinos. People who came to Africa thought the local people said white, not wide, and this is how they got their name.

An African white rhino

There are three sorts of rhinos living in Asia. These are the Indian, Sumatran and Javan rhino.

Indian rhinos live in open places, near rivers in the north of India and in Nepal.

The Sumatran rhino lives in forests in Borneo and Sumatra. It is sometimes called the hairy rhinoceros, because it has a shaggy coat of hair.

A Javan rhino

An Indian rhino

ASIAN RHINOS

A Sumatran rhino

All rhinos are herbivores, but different sorts of rhinos eat in different ways.

Grazers, such as the white rhinos in this picture, eat grass and other plants found on the ground.

Browsers, like the black rhino, eat leaves growing on bushes and trees.

Grazers and browsers have different shaped mouths. Wide mouths are good for grazing. Narrow, pointed lips are best for browsing.

A black rhino's mouth is the right shape for browsing.

FEEDING

RHINO LIFE

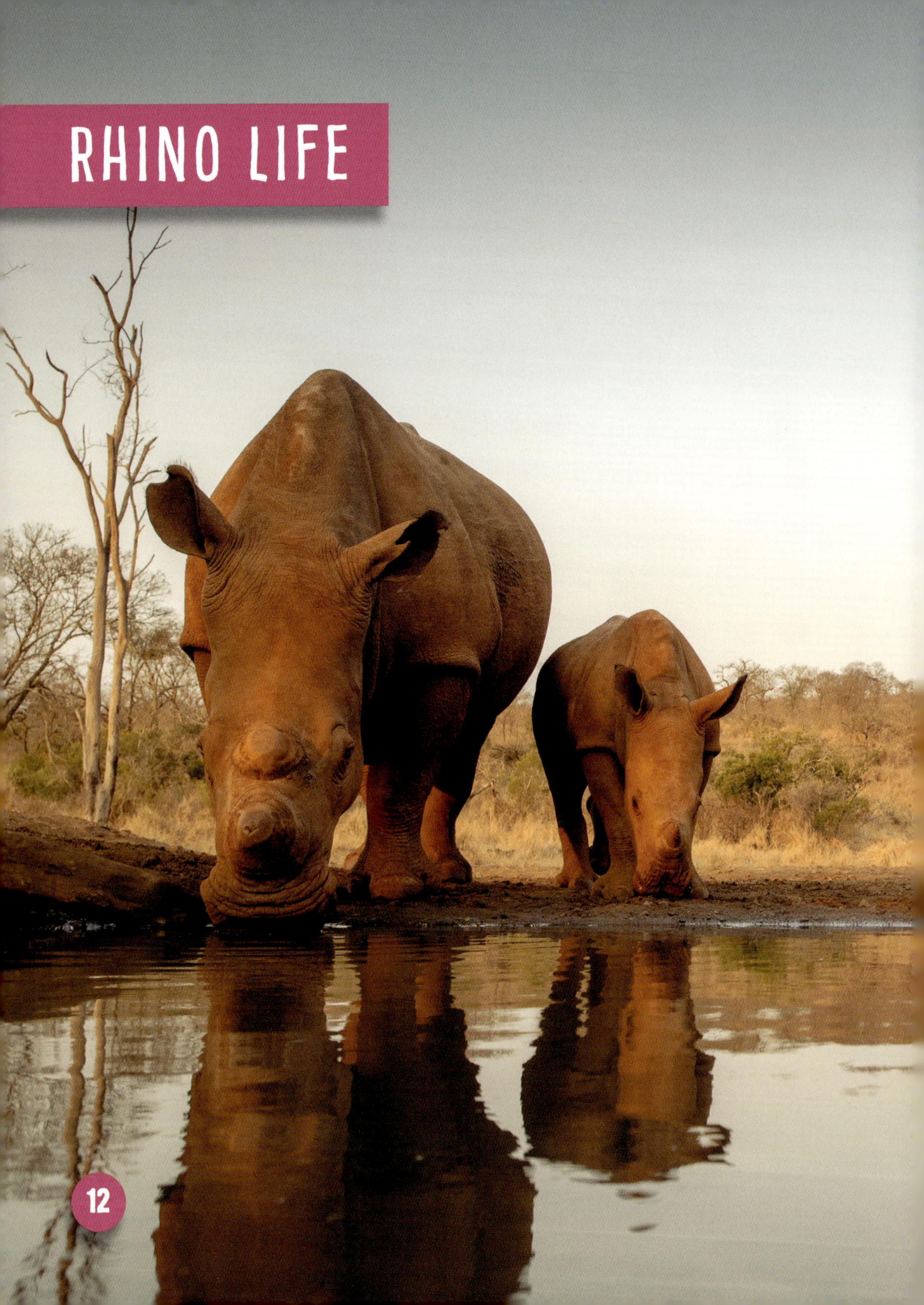

Adult rhinos usually live alone. They come together for mating and sometimes white rhinos will gather where there is lots of food or water.

If you see a group of rhinos, it is most likely to be a mom with her young, or a small group of females.

Male rhinos have **territories**. They mark them with piles of dung. Sometimes these are three feet (1 m) high! This is a warning to other male rhinos to stay away.

DID YOU KNOW?

Male rhinos will fight other male rhinos that come into their territory.

CHARGING RHINOS

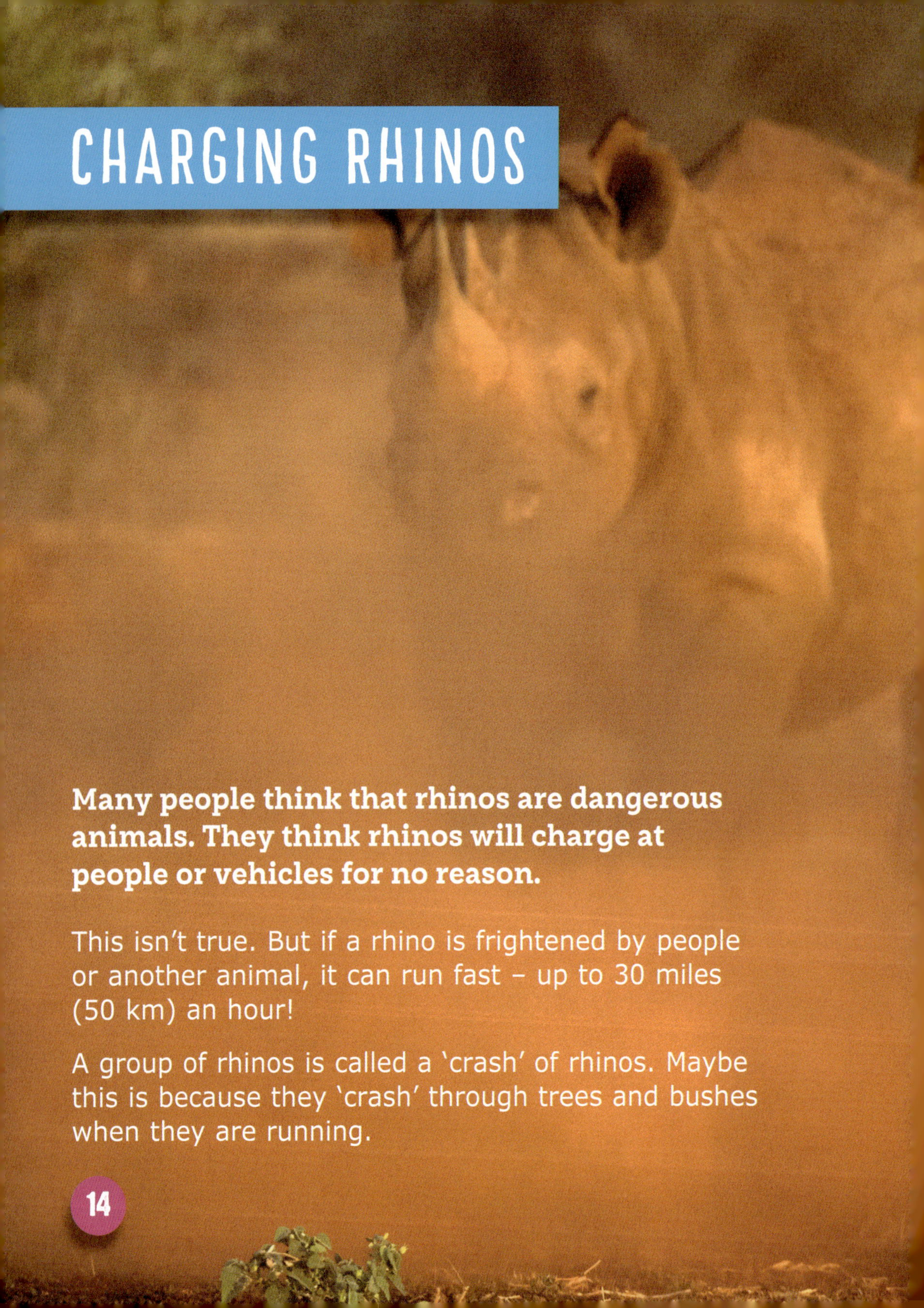

Many people think that rhinos are dangerous animals. They think rhinos will charge at people or vehicles for no reason.

This isn't true. But if a rhino is frightened by people or another animal, it can run fast – up to 30 miles (50 km) an hour!

A group of rhinos is called a 'crash' of rhinos. Maybe this is because they 'crash' through trees and bushes when they are running.

DID YOU KNOW?

White and Indian rhino calves run in front of their moms. Black, Javan and Sumatran rhino calves run behind their moms.

PROBLEMS: HORNS

DID YOU KNOW?

Rhino horns are made of keratin. This is the same stuff that your fingernails are made of.

Black and white rhinos and Sumatran rhinos have two horns. Indian and Javan rhinos have one horn.

Male rhinos use their horns when they are fighting over territories. The front horn of a male white rhino can grow to 50 inches (130 cm) long.

Some people use rhino horn to make medicines. They believe that it can cure illnesses – but this isn't true!

Rhino horn is also used to make dagger handles, called 'jambiya', in Yemen, Asia.

Many rhinos have been killed for their horns. **Poaching** is the main reason why these animals are endangered.

In Africa and in Asia, the human population is growing. More and more land is needed to grow food for people.

Rhinos need a large area of land to find enough food to eat. Their **habitat** is being taken over and used for farming.

Most rhinos now have to live in protected **wildlife reserves**.

In Asia, the Sumatran rhinos are losing their habitat too. The forests where they live are being cut down by **illegal loggers**.

PROBLEMS: HABITAT LOSS

Rhinos in an orphanage with rangers keeping an eye on them.

PROBLEMS: CLIMATE CHANGE

The changing climate could be a big problem for rhinos and other wild animals.

Climate change can cause **droughts**. Rhinos are put at risk if waterholes dry up. They have to travel long distances to find water, and might not find enough to survive!

When there is less rain, the sorts of plants that grow change. In Africa, the grasses that some rhinos eat might be replaced by scrubby bushes.

Less rain also means that desert areas with no plants at all will get bigger.

People are trying very hard to save the rhino.

Zoos around the world have set up **breeding programs** for rhinos.

In Africa and Asia wildlife reserves are meant to be safe homes for rhinos. Even so, sometimes poaching still happens.

One way to save the rhino is for **tourists** to visit the animals, to watch them in their natural habitat.

Wildlife tourism brings in money for the countries where rhinos live.

SAVING THE RHINO

FACT FILE

WHERE DO RHINOS LIVE?

The red areas on the maps show where rhinos live.

- Indian rhinos live in open areas in northern India and southern Nepal.
- Sumatran and Javan rhinos live in small areas of Nepal, Malaysia and Indonesia in swamps and forests.
- African rhinos live in eastern and southern Africa on open grasslands.

RHINO BODIES

White rhinos are the biggest of all the rhinos. After the elephant, they are the biggest land-living mammals.

THE BIGGEST:
White rhino
Length: up to 13 ft
Height: up to 6 ft
Weight: up to 5,500 lbs

THE SMALLEST:
Sumatran rhino
Length: up to 10 ft
Height: up to 5 ft
Weight: up to 1,750 lbs

- Both male and female rhinos have horns.
- Rhinos have big muscles in their neck to hold up their huge heads.
- Rhino skin looks tough, but it can be damaged by the sun and insect bites.

FACT FILE

RHINOS IN DANGER

While some rhino numbers are on the rise thanks to work by conservationists, many rhinos remain in serious danger of extinction.

- Javan and Sumatran rhinos are the most in danger. There are less than 100 of each species left in the wild.

A Javan rhino cub

- The biggest threats to rhinos are poaching and habitat loss.

- Rhino horns can be worth more than gold.

- Grassland habitat is being turned into farmland and forests are being cut down for wood.

FACT FILE

CONSERVATION

Conservationists are working hard to save rhinos. Thanks to their work, some rhino populations are beginning to recover.

- Wildlife reserves have been set up in Africa and India. Reserves have strong fences to keep poachers out, but this doesn't always work.

- Wildlife tourism can provide jobs and money for local people. This means that they are more likely to help protect the rhinos and their habitat.

- Conservationists are working to restore rhino habitats that have been destroyed.
- Some rhinos are being reintroduced into areas where they used to live.

HOW YOU CAN HELP

There are some great animal conservation charities and wildlife reserves that need money to pay for the work that they do. There are lots of fun ways that you could help to raise money and awareness for them.

- Why not organize a tasty bake sale?
- Ask people to sponsor you to do an activity. This could be something like a walk or a run, or helping to pick up trash in your local area.
- Put on a community or school event. How about a disco or a charity run?

Don't forget to get your family, friends and teachers involved! It'll be easier and much more fun with some help!

GLOSSARY

breeding programsww Zoos keep rare animals. They help them to breed by giving them mates, and they help to look after the babies. Many zoos try to put the animals they breed back into the wild, if it is safe.

climate change Rising global temperatures and changing weather patterns caused by a build up of gases in Earth's atmosphere.

conservationists People who take care of the natural world. Conservationists try to stop people hunting endangered animals and they ask governments to pass laws to protect wild habitats.

droughts When there is no rain for a very long time.

endangered At risk of becoming extinct.

extinct When a plant or animal no longer exists anywhere on Earth.

habitat The place that suits a particular animal or plant, in the wild.

herbivores Animals that live by eating plants.

illegal loggers People who cut down trees without permission to sell them for wood. They destroy large areas of forest habitat.

poaching The capturing or killing of animals by poachers so that they, or parts of their bodies, can be sold.

population A number of people or animals who live in a particular place or country.

savannah A large, open area of land in Africa where grasses and bushes grow.

territories Areas of land that one animal and its family believes is its own home and its area for finding its food.

tourists People who are visiting on vacation.

wildlife reserves Places set aside for wild animals and plants to live. The animals and their habitat are protected by laws.

INDEX